The
Seaside
Puppy

The Seaside Puppy

Holly Webb
Illustrated by Sophy Williams

stripes

For Eva

www.hollywebbanimalstories.com

STRIPES PUBLISHING LIMITED
An imprint of the Little Tiger Group
1 Coda Studios, 189 Munster Road,
London SW6 6AW

A paperback original
First published in Great Britain in 2016

Text copyright © Holly Webb, 2016
Illustrations copyright © Sophy Williams, 2016
Author photograph copyright © Nigel Bird

ISBN: 978-1-84715-652-5

A CIP catalogue record for this book is available
from the British Library.

Printed and bound in the UK.

10 9 8 7 6

Chapter One

"Are you going on holiday?" Max asked, whacking at a clump of nettles with a stick as they walked home from school along the lane. "We're going to Spain on Saturday."

"Yes, we are, but not until September, just before we go back to school," Jessie said. "We're going to Scotland for a week, to stay with my gran."

"We can't," Laura said, a little sadly. Almost everybody in her class seemed to be going somewhere amazing, but she was staying at home all summer. She gave a tiny sigh and peered over the bramble bushes to catch a glimpse of the sea. It was really blue, and the sun was making the ripples glitter. Laura knew they were lucky to live in such a beautiful place, but it would have been nice to go on holiday somewhere different!

"Mum's working," Laura went on. "It's the busiest time of year for her, the summer. All the cottages are booked up for the whole seven weeks. She says she's going to be run off her feet."

Jessie nodded. "Never mind. I'll be around until the end of August.

We can go to the beach. Mum's booked me some bodyboarding lessons for the first couple of weeks. I want to get lots of practice in."

Max snorted. "Yeah, you *need* the practice."

Jessie blew a cloud of dandelion seeds at him, so they caught in his blond hair, coating it in white fluff. It made him look about sixty years older all of a sudden.

"Oi, get them off me! Uurrgh." Max flailed at his hair crossly. "They're all itchy."

"Serves you right," Laura pointed out. "Just because you've been surfing since you could stand up, doesn't mean you have to be horrible to Jessie. She's only lived here a year!" She smiled gratefully at Jessie – she was really glad that someone was going to be around for most of the summer.

Lots of their friends lived quite a long way from Tremarren and travelled in by the school bus, so it wasn't that simple to meet up with them in the holidays. Mum had promised Laura that they'd try to fit in some fun treats and go to the beach together, but Laura knew how busy she would be. Laura didn't like seeing her so tired. Managing the cottages meant that Mum was on duty twenty-four hours a day, really, in case any of the guests had a problem.

Laura helped out as much as she could, although mostly she sat and did her homework while Mum was cleaning the cottages. But this holiday, now Laura was nearly ten, they'd agreed that she was old enough to stay at home while Mum was out. The holiday cottages and the little cottage where she and Mum lived had all been converted from the old farm buildings, so Mum would never be that far away. Since the beginning of term, she'd let Laura walk to and from school with Max and Jessie. Laura was even allowed to go to the beach for a little bit by herself or with friends. She wasn't allowed to swim on her own, though.

Mum had made her promise.

The best thing was that over the last few weeks, Mum had let her go to the village by herself to do some of the shopping. Laura had been begging for ages – after all, everyone in the shops knew her, she'd told Mum. It made a big difference, Mum not having to do all the shopping as well as everything else. Laura loved seeing her come home and look in the fridge, and say how nice it was to have everything done.

They were coming into the village now, and Jessie and Max waved goodbye as they headed down their road. Laura had to go on a little bit – Tremarren Farm, where she lived, was just on the other side of the village.

Laura sped up as she saw Mrs Eccles out for a walk with her Jack Russell, Toby. Mrs Eccles had been Laura's Reception teacher. She'd retired a couple of years ago and got Toby to keep her company.

"Hello, Laura! It's the last day of school, isn't it?" Mrs Eccles called. "Are you excited about the holidays?"

Laura crouched down to stroke Toby's ears. He was such a sweet dog, even though Mrs Eccles said he was really naughty and a terrible thief.

"Don't fuss over that little horror too much," she said to Laura. "He ate my breakfast this morning. A whole piece of toast! I don't think he even chewed it – it just went straight down his throat. Little monster, aren't you?"

11

she told Toby lovingly, and he sat
there beating his tail hard against the
pavement. He loved being petted, and
Laura was one of his favourite people.

"Oh, you bad dog," Laura
murmured, scratching under his chin.
"You'll get fat!"

"Luckily he goes three times as far as I do whenever we're out for a walk, what with all the dashing around, sniffing and chasing butterflies," Mrs Eccles said. "We're going all the way to the lighthouse this afternoon. He can work off that toast! See you soon, Laura. Have a brilliant first day of the holidays!"

Laura waved as Mrs Eccles and Toby turned down the side street that led to the cliff path. A lovely long walk all the way to the lighthouse with gorgeous Toby... She watched enviously as they disappeared round the corner. Walks were so much more fun with a dog. She'd seen Toby chasing sticks and Frisbees, jumping in and out of the sea and barking at the waves. Maybe Mrs Eccles would let her come along with them at some point over the holidays? Laura nodded to herself. She'd ask Mrs Eccles, the next time she saw them.

Henry padded uncertainly through the house, sniffing at the furniture. He didn't understand what was happening. He felt dizzy and a bit sick from being in the car for so long. And when they'd got out they weren't back home. They were somewhere else.

But at least Annie was here. She was rushing around with the others, up and down the stairs, throwing doors open. They kept shouting. One of the boys had tripped over Henry and then trodden on his tail – so now the puppy was keeping out of the way. Perhaps this was his new home, he thought worriedly, sitting down under the kitchen table in a forest of chair legs.

"Hey, Henry!" Annie crouched down to pat him. "Are you all right? Did you find your basket? Here, look."

Henry followed her over to the corner of the kitchen and sniffed obediently at his basket. Fortunately *that* was the same.

Annie put down a bowl of water, which he drank eagerly. But when he looked up she'd disappeared again, and his ears drooped. He climbed into the basket, slumped down with his muzzle sticking out over the dipped edge, and waited.

He wasn't really sure what he was waiting for. A walk? For Annie to come back and pick him up? He lay there, listening, his ears flicking. Every so often he thumped his tail on his cushioned basket when he heard someone come past. But no one stopped to fuss over him. Eventually, Henry drifted off to sleep.

Chapter Two

"I'm a bit worried about that big group in the old farmhouse." Laura's mum sighed. "I've just been over to check how they're settling in. The whole house is in a mess already, and they've only just arrived. Bags and clothes all over the place! I don't think any of them are more than eighteen. They're having a holiday together because they've all just finished their exams, I imagine."

"Are they staying long?" Laura asked, pouring milk over her cereal. She was still in her pyjamas, looking forward to a lazy breakfast with no need to rush off to school.

"A whole fortnight!" Mum rolled her eyes. "I suppose it means less fuss changing over the farmhouse for another family after a week, but I do wish they were a bit more sensible." She sighed again, and then smiled at Laura. "They've brought a very cute little dog with them, though. He's a spaniel, I think. I'm sure you'd know, Laura."

Laura sat up straighter and peered out of the kitchen window, wondering if she might see the little dog.

The old farmhouse was the biggest of the holiday homes, and it was just across the pretty paved yard from Laura and her mum's cottage. The farmhouse was right next to the lane that led down to the beach and it had amazing views of the sea. It was always booked solid in the holidays. But right now the whole house looked quiet. All the curtains were still drawn and there was certainly no sign of a dog.

Mum laughed. "So you're going to spend the whole day staring out of the window to see if they go for a walk, are you?"

"No…" Laura said, going back to her cereal. But secretly she was thinking that it wouldn't be all that difficult to accidentally-on-purpose run into the dog and his owner.

Later that afternoon, Laura was shooting a ball at the basketball hoop in the courtyard when she heard a door closing behind her and a boy's loud voice.

"Come on, Henry! Get a move on!"

Laura looked round, wondering who Henry was and feeling a bit sorry for him. Then she gave a delighted gasp.

A beautiful King Charles spaniel was sniffing at the huge flowerpots on either side of the farmhouse door. He was only a puppy, Laura thought – he was really little. He bounced about on spindly short legs, yipping excitedly and whisking his fluffy ears. Mum had been right about his breed. Laura had seen King Charles spaniels before, but never a tiny puppy like this one. She giggled as she spotted his big ginger eyebrows. They gave his face such a sweet grumpy look.

"Oh, he's gorgeous. How old is he?" Laura asked, hurrying over to the teenage boy who was pulling at the puppy's lead. She was sure that someone who was walking such a lovely dog would be happy to talk about him. Who wouldn't want to show off a puppy like that?

"What?" the boy said, staring at her. His voice didn't sound very friendly, and Laura went pink.

"I-I just wondered how old he was?" she stuttered. "He looks very small."

"Haven't a clue. Come on, Henry, stop messing around." The boy tugged at the puppy's lead, and finally

22

managed to drag him away from the flowerpots and out into the yard.

The puppy pulled back against his collar, whining a little, and Laura bit her lip. She wanted to tell the boy not to yank at his neck like that – that he was hurting him. But she wasn't quite brave enough. The puppy, Henry, belonged to this boy, or at least to one of his friends. She didn't have any right to tell him off.

Then the puppy seemed to catch the scent of the sea. He sniffed deeply and his ears twitched, and he followed the boy quite happily round the corner of the farmhouse, towards the path that led down to the beach. Laura watched them go, then slowly walked back over to her cottage.

Henry sat up and yawned, then peered over the edge of his basket. It was still much too large for him, but his toys helped to fill up the rest of the space.

He stared over at the kitchen door and heaved a great sigh. Then he nosed thoughtfully at his squashy ball, pushing it against the side of the basket. It let out a faint squeak and he patted at it with his paw – but it wasn't as much fun without someone to throw it for him.

Henry gazed over at the door again. Where were they? He'd been asleep for ages, he was sure. And he needed to go out… He'd had a short walk earlier on with one of the boys, just down the lane a little way. There hadn't been time for any proper exploring, but at least he'd had the chance to do a wee. Now he definitely needed to go again. He knew he shouldn't wee in the house – and there wasn't even any newspaper down. But he just couldn't wait any longer.

Henry climbed out of his basket, looking around uncertainly. Then he made a puddle and hurried away from it guiltily.

He was starting to feel hungry, too. It was such a long time since breakfast. He was used to three meals a day, and now that he thought about it, he felt miserably empty. He went pattering around the kitchen, sniffing for something to eat. He scrabbled at the door of the cupboard where he'd seen Annie put his bag of dog food, but it didn't open.

Slowly he wandered out of the kitchen and into the big living room. There were bags and clothes scattered around on the floor and over the sofas, and he wondered if some of them might have food in. One red handbag smelled delicious. A sweet, rich smell – much nicer than his dog food. The bag was zipped shut, though, and however hard he scrabbled at the fabric, he couldn't get in.

Henry sat back and looked at it. He was hungrier than ever now. He felt as though he could just eat the whole bag… He wagged his feathery tail briskly and crouched down by the side of the handbag, baring his sharp little teeth. It only took a few minutes to chew through the side and pull out a packet of biscuits. The plastic caught in his teeth as he tore the packet open, but Henry didn't mind too much.

He gobbled up the whole lot, then stretched happily and flopped down on top of the squashy red bag for a sleep. All that biting at the tough fabric had worn him out.

Chapter Three

Henry's ears twitched a little as he heard voices and footsteps, and then the door banging.

"Look at my bag!"

Henry woke up properly with a start. Someone was shouting. He could almost feel the noise, as if the air was shaking. With a tiny whimper, he pressed himself down into the soft fabric of his basket. Were they shouting at him?

"That stupid dog! He's ruined it. Look, it's chewed to bits!"

"Oh, Molly. I'm really sorry. Henry, you bad dog! Bad dog!"

Annie had crouched down next to the basket, and she said the words in a loud, cross voice – not at all like the voice she normally used.

Henry whimpered again. It was definitely him they were cross with. But why? Annie never spoke to him like that. He quivered his tail, just a little, to show he was sorry, but she didn't seem to notice.

He watched miserably as Annie stood up and turned to the other girl, looking at the bag he'd eaten the biscuits from earlier on that day. She pulled out the chewed-up scraps of packet and sighed. "I guess it's my fault. He was hungry – I should have given him something before we went out. I'll get you a new bag, Molly!"

Annie put her arm round Molly's shoulders and led her out into the garden. Henry watched them go, his ears drooping. Those biscuits seemed a long time ago...

"I had a feeling that group of teenagers were going to be difficult," Laura's mum sighed as she put her phone away. "That was the lady who's staying in Rose Cottage. She said they were still out in the garden at midnight, shouting and playing music."

Laura looked at her in surprise. "I didn't hear anything."

Mum shook her head. "No, I didn't, either, but I suppose if we were already asleep, we might not have done. And the garden's behind the farmhouse, between it and Rose Cottage. So the noise probably travelled that way."

"I hope Henry wasn't scared by the noise," Laura murmured.

"Henry? Oh, the little dog. Is that what he's called?" Mum smiled. "I might have known you'd find that out."

"I saw one of the boys taking him for a walk," Laura explained. "He's so cute – he's really tiny. I don't think that boy liked him very much, though," she added, frowning as she remembered. "He just kept telling him to come on, and yanking at his lead."

"Oh dear… Perhaps it wasn't his dog." The phone suddenly shrilled

again and Mum pulled it out of
her pocket, looking at it anxiously.
"Hello? Oh, hello. I see. No, that's
not good. And you took him back?
Well, thank you. Yes, of course, I'll
have a word with them. Thanks
so much."

She ended the call and rolled her
eyes at Laura.
"*That* was the
family from
High Cliffs
Cottage.
They've
just found
a little dog in
their kitchen, eating
their lunch!"

"What?" Laura blinked at her.

"They'd left their back door open and he just walked in. They found him standing on the kitchen table, eating a plate of sandwiches."

Laura giggled. It *was* quite funny. But poor Henry! The man on the phone had sounded really annoyed. She'd heard him even from across the kitchen table and she was worried he would have yelled at the puppy. Henry had probably got a horrible shock.

"I think I'd better go over to High Cliffs and make sure everything else is all right," Mum said. "They were kind enough to take Henry back to the farmhouse, but they weren't pleased. And then I suppose I'd better go and talk to his owner." She sighed.

"You'll be all right here, won't you, Laura? Maybe when I get back we could go and have a game of table tennis." She gave Laura a hug. "I'm sorry, sweetheart. I was hoping we'd be able to spend some time together today, as we haven't really had a chance since school broke up."

"It's OK," Laura said. "I might go for a walk along the clifftop. Max said there was going to be a lifeboat display this afternoon, with a rescue helicopter. I can go and watch from the path. Though probably he got the day wrong, knowing Max!"

Mum laughed. "OK. I'll see you in a bit. Have fun!"

Laura grabbed her little rucksack and slipped in an apple for a snack, along with a water bottle – it felt even hotter this afternoon. Then she let herself out of the front door. Of course, taking the cliff path meant going straight past the farmhouse…

She was worried about Henry. That boy walking him yesterday had sounded really grumpy. And now the little puppy had been running loose! Surely his owners hadn't just let him out, had they? Laura chewed her lip anxiously. Either Henry had been let out on purpose, or he'd slipped away and they hadn't even noticed that he was gone. She wasn't sure which was worse.

As Laura walked across the yard,

one of the girls from the farmhouse came round the corner and smiled at her. She had very bright blue eyes and curly dark hair, and she looked really friendly. Laura smiled back.

"You live here, don't you?" the older girl asked her. "You're so lucky! I can't imagine living somewhere so beautiful all year round."

"It is nice," Laura agreed. "Pretty cold and windy in the winter, though. Are you here because it's the end of your exams?"

"Mm-hm. We're all friends from school. I'm Annie, by the way."

"I'm Laura," Laura told her, a little shyly. "I saw the dog who's staying with you at the farmhouse yesterday. He's so sweet."

Annie rolled her eyes. "He's mine. He is sweet, but he's been really naughty since we got here. I suppose it's just a bit strange for him, being in a new place. He chewed up my friend Molly's handbag – she was furious. And then this morning I didn't get round to taking him out before we went food shopping, and he went walkabout. Poor Henry. It's a bit of a pain that we can't bring him to the beach with us. Logan took him out for a walk yesterday, but he's been stuck here at the house since.

I think maybe he's bored."

"Oh but you can take dogs on most of the beach," Laura explained. "Just not Gull Cove – that's the part closest to the village."

"Oh, OK. That's the nice sandy bit, though, isn't it?"

"Well, if…" Laura gulped nervously, then decided that the worst thing Annie could say to her was no. "If you think Henry needs some exercise while you're out, maybe I could take him for a walk along the beach here."

Annie stared at her. "Really?"

"Yeah. I love dogs and I don't have one. I'd like to. Um, if you think that would be OK."

"Sure." Annie beamed at her. "That would be great. You can take him now, if you like? I'll go and get him."

"Oh!" Laura nodded eagerly. "Right now? Yes, please!"

Annie grinned at her and headed into the farmhouse, while Laura waited in the yard. She was so excited she was actually hopping from foot to foot, she realized. She went pink and put both feet very firmly on the ground. Annie wouldn't want her to take Henry out if she thought Laura was being silly.

Laura knew she ought to go and tell her mum, but she squashed down the thought at the back of her mind. Mum had gone off to talk to the people at High Cliffs Cottage, so she couldn't ask right now. And Laura was pretty sure Mum wouldn't mind. After all, she'd said that Henry was really cute, hadn't she?

Then Annie came out with Henry, and all thoughts about asking Mum went out of Laura's head entirely. He was just so lovely. He was peeping shyly round Annie's legs, looking up at Laura with his head on one side. A smart red collar and lead stood out against the black fur of his neck, and his white paws were spotlessly clean.

Laura crouched down and slowly put out one hand for Henry to sniff.

"You're sure it's all right for me to take him?" Laura said, as the puppy eyed her cautiously.

"Of course." Annie put the lead into Laura's hand and patted Henry. "Be good, Henry-dog! Oh! Nearly forgot." She darted back into the house. "You might need these. Poo bags." She made a face. "I know it's a bit disgusting…"

Laura shook her head. "No. I mean, it is, but it would be worse just leaving it for someone to tread in. Thanks." She tucked the bags in her pocket and looked down at the puppy. "Going to come for a walk, Henry?" Then she giggled as Henry's tail began to sweep from side to side, faster and faster.

He obviously knew what that word meant. She tugged gently on his lead and set off around the side of the farmhouse, down the path to the clifftop and the beach.

Henry followed, a little confused by this new person. But then he'd seen a lot of new people over the last few days. The house was full of strange, big, noisy people. Whenever he was settling down to sleep, or trying to climb on Annie's lap for a cuddle, someone would clomp by loudly, or fling themselves down on to the sofa.

He trotted after the girl, liking the low voice she was using to coax him along and the way she didn't pull at his lead.

The narrow path that led to the cliffs was a bit overgrown, but it smelled amazing to a small dog. Henry stopped to plunge his nose among the clumps of grass, shaking his feathery ears in excitement. He snorted delightedly, snuffling in among the weeds, and the girl laughed.

"Is that nice?" she murmured. "What can you smell? Is it rabbits?"

Henry looked up at her, wagging his tail, and then licked her hand. The sun was warm on his fur and the air was full of good smells. This girl wasn't hurrying him along like that boy, Logan, had the day before. She didn't seem to mind how long he spent investigating everything. He panted happily and headed on down the path.

Chapter Four

Laura looked down at Henry thoughtfully. He was prancing along, although he did keep stopping to sniff at something every couple of metres, which slowed them down a bit. Even though he was so bouncy, she wasn't sure how far he'd be able to walk. She knew King Charles spaniels could be energetic, but he was only little – and she didn't think that Annie had been taking him on long walks, either.

"We'd better not go too far," she said. "Let's walk down the path to the beach. This is Warren Cove. I bet you smelled all the rabbits up on the cliff, didn't you?"

Henry scurried down the path ahead of her, ears flapping in the breeze. As the scrubby grass turned to sand and pebbles he stopped, lifting up each front paw, and then putting them down again, looking confused. This gritty stuff between his paws was new, his expression said quite clearly.

"Haven't you been on the beach at all?" Laura said, surprised. "Oh, of course – they thought you weren't allowed.

It's sand. Don't you like it? You can dig, look." She crouched down and scuffled a hole in the sand, just in front of Henry's nose. He gave a squeaky little yelp and plunged both forepaws in straight away, scratching madly and sending sand flying all over the place.

Laura sat back, laughing and holding up her hand to shield her face. "I'm going to have to brush you before I give you back – you're covered!"

The puppy's long fur was clotted with golden biscuity sand, especially in the pretty feathery bits around his paws and chest.

"Unless you wanted to go for a paddle, of course," Laura said, looking thoughtfully at the sea. It was beautifully calm today – a still, glassy greenish-blue, with little creamy waves breaking on to the pebbles. "Come on, Henry. Let's go and have a look at the sea." She jumped up, patting at her leg, and Henry trotted after her.

Henry slowed down as they got closer to the water and stared at it suspiciously.

"It's OK," Laura whispered, kicking off her flip-flops and

crouching down next to him. "I know, it's funny, isn't it? It keeps going in and out."

Henry looked up at her and wagged his tail uncertainly. He didn't understand what the sea was at all. But the girl didn't sound very worried by it. She didn't step back when it came hissing and foaming towards them.

Laura stayed crouching next to Henry. She hoped he would go into the water – she knew lots of dogs loved swimming. It would wash some of the sand off, too. And she couldn't help imagining how gorgeous he'd look, paddling about in the sea… She didn't want to make him, though.

Henry took a step forward, and then barked in surprise as the water made a rush at him, sucking the sand out from beneath his paws. It was cold! He shook his paws, then barked again as the drops splashed and sparkled around him.

Laura giggled, and he looked up at her. "Do you like it?" she asked. She couldn't quite tell.

Henry stayed put, even though the next wave came right up to his tummy. He jumped and barked at the ripples and the yellowish foam.

Laura was just thinking how much fun it would be to come down with her swimming costume on one day, so she and Henry could have a proper splash about, when a sudden loud roaring made her jump. She nearly slipped over, but then she clapped a hand over her mouth and laughed. "Oh! Oh, wow, a helicopter!"

It was flying round the curve of the cliffs that shaped the little bay and divided the two beaches. The tall cliffs had shielded Laura and Henry from the sound of the rotors until it came right into the bay.

"I guess it's on the way to that lifeboat display Max was talking about," Laura said.

The lead suddenly jerked in her hands

and Laura looked down in surprise.
"Oh, Henry!"

The puppy was whining in fright,
tugging frantically at the lead and
backing away across the sand.

He hated the noise. He'd never
heard anything so loud and he could
feel the ground shaking.

"Don't worry." Laura
picked him up, hugging
the tiny dog tight.
He was really scared,
she could tell – he
was shivering in her
arms. "Honestly, it's just
a helicopter. It was noisy,
though wasn't it?" She went on
talking soothing nonsense to calm him
down as the helicopter flew across the bay.

At last it disappeared round the other side of the cliffs. "It's gone now," she said gently. "Come on, sweetie. Do you want to paddle a bit more?" She rubbed her hand over his silky ears and he snuggled against her, burying his head in her T-shirt.

"Maybe we'd better just head home," Laura muttered, grabbing her flip-flops and wobbling as she tried to put them back on without letting go of Henry. "I don't know if that helicopter's going to come past again." She picked her way slowly across the stones towards the steps that led up from the other end of the beach.

Henry wriggled in her arms as he picked up the scent of a patch of half-dried seaweed. Laura thought it smelled disgusting, but she supposed it might be nice if you were a dog. She put him down so he could rootle through it. At least it was distracting him from the scary helicopter.

Finally Henry lost interest in the seaweed and went sniffing his way across the beach towards the path. He was still a bit twitchy, Laura noticed. When he heard another dog barking from up on the cliffs, he jumped and pressed himself against her legs.

Laura went on murmuring to him as they walked up the cliff path – saying comforting things about how nice the hot sun was, and how she loved the sharp smell of the wild fennel growing along the path. She could see he was listening to her. Of course he didn't understand what she was saying, but Laura was sure that didn't matter.

They stopped at the top and Laura let out a great sigh. "That path is so steep!" She glanced down at Henry, who was panting, too. He flopped on to the short turf, looking tired and hot.

"You need a drink," Laura said, sitting down beside him and opening up her rucksack. She looked at her water bottle, wondering if Henry would let her dribble some water in his mouth. She wished she'd thought of bringing him a bowl. Henry was still panting, with fast, short little breaths. He sounded miserable.

"This will have to do," Laura told him, cupping one hand and pouring some water into it. She saw Henry's ears flickering as he heard the splashing sound, and he sat up eagerly. She held her hand under his nose, and at first he just looked at it, confused. Then he realized what she was doing and lapped eagerly at the water. It was gone in seconds.

"More?" Laura refilled her hand, giggling as Henry's soft pink tongue swept over her palm. "You really are thirsty."

Henry drank five handfuls of water, and then flopped down again. But this time he looked much happier. He was resting his chin on his paws as he watched the bees buzzing through the wild flowers by the path.

Laura sat stroking his back, feeling the sun on her hair and pretending, just for a moment, that Henry was hers.

"I'd take you on lots of walks," she whispered. "Of course I'd always bring your water bowl. And I'd never let a helicopter come anywhere near." She smiled to herself. As if she could stop a helicopter! But it was all just imagining, anyway. Henry was someone else's puppy.

"I suppose we ought to get going," Laura sighed at last. "Come on, Henry. It isn't too far, I promise."

Henry heaved himself up and padded along the grassy path after Laura. He wasn't as bouncy as he had been when they'd set off, but he still looked like he was enjoying himself. When a butterfly fluttered over his nose he yapped excitedly and tried to jump up at it. He didn't get anywhere near, of course, and he watched rather grumpily as the butterfly whirled away.

Laura laughed. "You are a funny thing," she told him. "What would you do with a butterfly if you caught it, anyway?"

They were almost home when a couple of seagulls came diving by. Huge white herring gulls with wide grey wings. They swooped over Laura and Henry, shrieking, and Henry squealed in fright. He was still a bit nervous from before, and the gulls had darted straight past his nose!

"Henry!" Laura yelled in panic as the puppy tugged hard at his lead and it slipped out of her hand.

She dashed after him as he turned tail and raced back along the path the way they'd come. He didn't stop until he came to a tangle of brambles, just at the edge of the cliff. The stems were thick and dark with thorns, but he wriggled underneath.

Laura kneeled down to look at him,

crouching under the brambles. "Oh, Henry," she whispered.

The puppy peered out at her and whimpered a little. Everything was different and scary, and he didn't understand. First the new house and all those people who kept shouting at him. Then that roaring thing had swooped over his head, so loud it had made his ears hurt. And now the shrieking birds. Everything felt wrong.

"It's all right…" The girl was talking again, so quietly. Her whispers were soothing and he crept out of the brambles a little, just close enough for her to rub her hand over his head and stroke his ears.

He crawled a bit further, plunging his head into her knees and letting her wrap her arms around him. She smelled good, Henry thought. His racing heart slowed slightly and he relaxed against her with a shiver.

"Poor Henry," she muttered. "Poor sweetheart. You're safe now."

Chapter Five

"She really lets you take him for a walk every day?" Jessie asked, wonderingly.

"Every day for the last five days now. I'm so lucky. We went as far as the lighthouse this morning. That's a long walk for him, but he was brilliant." Laura smiled down proudly at Henry as he pranced over the sand in front of them. "I didn't think Annie would ever let me take him out again after the first time. He was all sandy and he had bits of bramble in his fur when we got back. But she went and got his brush, and we groomed him together. Annie said he seemed to really like me."

"Yes, but why doesn't she want to take him herself?" Jessie asked. "If I had a gorgeous dog like that, I wouldn't let other people walk him!"

"I suppose she doesn't have time because she's on holiday with her friends. I don't know – I'm just grateful." Laura sighed. "But I'm going to miss him so much when they go. They're only here for one more week. Of course, Mum can't wait for them to leave. Two of the other families have complained that they're too noisy, and she keeps worrying about what's going to go wrong next!"

"Oh yes, she was telling my mum about them when they ran into each other in the baker's. Is your mum OK with you going off walking him all the time?"

"She said it was fine as long as I tell her where we're going. But she was a bit worried when I told her about those seagulls."

Jessie shuddered. "One of them snatched my sandwich last summer when we were having a picnic on the beach. They're huge!"

"Especially when you're only the size of Henry," Laura agreed.

They both laughed as Henry stopped and turned round. It was like he understood that they were talking about him.

"Did you tell Annie about the seagulls, too?" Jessie said.

Laura nodded. "I didn't really want to, in case she thought I wasn't looking after him properly, but I had to explain all those bits of bramble in his fur."

"So what did she say?" Jessie asked.

Laura ruffled Henry's ears. "She said she wasn't very surprised. She should have warned me he hated loud noises, and it definitely wasn't my fault he slipped the lead. Oh, look, that's her," Laura said, nudging Jessie. "With the curly hair. I thought they always went to Gull Cove."

"If they were coming here, she could have taken Henry with her. After all, dogs are allowed on this beach," Jessie pointed out.

Laura shrugged – she wasn't sure

why Annie hadn't brought him, either. "I suppose he wouldn't want to sit still while they all sunbathed…"

Annie was lying on the sand and chatting with one of the other girls from the farmhouse, the one Laura thought was called Molly. Laura had met her when she took Henry back the day before.

Annie sat up as she saw them coming over and shielded her eyes from the sun. "Hi there, Laura! Hi, Henry!"

Henry scampered over to her excitedly, pulling Laura along behind him. He ran across Annie's towel and scrabbled at her, hoping she'd fuss over him.

"Ow, ow, claws!" Annie pushed him away gently. She was only wearing a swimming costume and he was scratching her legs.

Henry sat back, his ears drooping a little, and Laura crouched down to stroke him. "It's OK – you can't jump up on people, that's all," she said. But she felt bad for the puppy. He'd just wanted his owner to give him a cuddle.

Henry wagged his tail slowly as she stroked him, and Annie kneeled up and joined in.

"You're so good with him," Annie told Laura, ruffling Henry's ears.

"Thanks!" Laura smiled at her. "I think he's the nicest dog I've ever met. Jessie thinks he's beautiful, too."

"And really friendly," Jessie added.

Annie smiled. "I know – he's perfect."

"You have to be quiet," Laura whispered. "Mum's out, and I don't think she'll be back for a while, but just in case." She watched happily as Henry sniffed his way around her bedroom. He spent ages nosing at her trainers, and Laura made faces at him. "That's disgusting! Yuck!"

Henry sat back and sneezed, looking very surprised at himself. Laura laughed so much she had to hug her arms tight around her ribs to stop them hurting. His ginger eyebrows looked as if they might lift off! But after one last quick sniff at the trainers, he went on exploring, scrabbling at Laura's bin to see what was inside. He had his front paws balanced on the edge as he kicked and scrambled his back paws up the side.

"Hey, Henry, that's going to tip over," Laura started to say, hopping up from her bed, but the bin had already started falling. Henry collapsed on the floor in a pile of screwed up homework sheets.

"You do look funny, silly dog," Laura told him, stuffing all the paper back into the bin and scooping him up for a cuddle. "Come on, come and sit with me on the bed."

It was so hot today, too hot and sticky to be outside in the sun, Laura thought. Especially for a little puppy. So she'd retreated to her room instead. She was sure Annie wouldn't mind her taking Henry up there.

Henry snuggled happily in Laura's lap and she leaned back against the pile of cushions and soft toys. It was so warm, even with the skylight and windows open. Henry turned himself around a couple of times, yawned hugely and slumped down again. He still had that puppy knack of falling asleep in seconds, whatever he was doing.

Laura looked down at Henry lovingly and stretched out one arm to grab the book from her bedside table. She didn't want to disturb him, he looked so comfy. She'd just read for a bit...

"Laura!"

Laura sat up with a jerk, and Henry started to slide off her lap. As she grabbed at him, he snuffled and snorted and woke up, looking surprised.

Laura gaped up at her mum. She'd fallen asleep! They both had! She'd meant to take Henry home long before

Mum was due back. She hoped Annie wasn't too worried.

"Sorry," she said. "I should have asked…"

Her mum sat down beside her on the bed and tickled Henry under the chin. He wagged his tail happily and stomped across the bed to give Mum a proper sniff. Then he slumped down again, still weary, with his chin on her leg.

"Aww," Laura's mum sighed, stroking his ears. "But I'm still cross with you, Laura," she added quickly. "Yes, you *definitely* should have asked. And I'd probably have said no."

"Don't you like him?" Laura said, rather sadly.

"Of course I like him – he's adorable. But he's not yours. That's what worries me.

You've been spending so much time with him, and now he's in your bedroom – just like he's your own puppy! He'll be going home soon, and I don't want you to be upset."

Laura's shoulders slumped. "I know he'll go home with Annie. And I already know how much I'll miss him," she admitted in a whisper. "But at least he's happy here with me. I'm not sure Annie's looking after him very well," she added. "If I didn't walk him, Mum, I don't know if anybody would. They always leave him in the house on his own when they go to the beach. They could easily take him with them."

Mum leaned back against the cushions and looked at Henry. "It's really good that you care about him so much," she said slowly, "but there's not a lot we can do. He belongs to someone else. He's Annie's dog, Laura."

"People who are lucky enough to have dogs ought to take better care of them!" Laura burst out. Her eyes were shining with tears, but her fists were clenched and she looked more angry than upset.

Henry gazed up at her and hunched his shoulders anxiously. He could hear the unhappiness in her voice and he let out a tiny whimper.

"I'm sorry, Henry. I didn't mean to scare you." Laura ran her hand gently over his head, murmuring to him soothingly.

Henry padded round in a circle on the bed, and then scrambled back into her lap and settled down. He was still eyeing Laura cautiously, though. He loved her partly for her quiet, gentle voice. That high, angry tone was all wrong – he'd never heard her sound like that before.

Henry wasn't sure what had happened. He liked the lady sitting next to them, too – she'd stroked him and made a fuss of him. But then something she'd said had made Laura's voice go sharp. Now he looked between Laura and her mum uncertainly.

"He's very quick at picking up how people feel, isn't he?" Mum murmured. "He knew straight away that you were upset and he didn't like it."

"I know… I think he doesn't like how busy and loud the farmhouse is, either," Laura said, glancing up at her worriedly. "When I took him back there yesterday, after our walk with Jessie, a couple of the boys were shouting. They weren't fighting or anything, just yelling because one was upstairs and one was downstairs, but Henry really flinched. He squashed himself down so he was practically on the floor."

"Well, I suppose it isn't for much longer." Mum put her arm round Laura's shoulders. "I'm sorry, Laura, but you know what I mean. If he isn't happy in that noisy house, he'll be better off back at home, won't he?"

"Yes, you're right." Laura's head drooped.

"Listen –" Mum hugged her tighter – "I don't think we could now, not when it's summer and I'm working so much, but maybe later in the year…"

Laura looked at her, confused, and Mum laughed. "What I'm trying to say

is – would you like us to get a dog of
our own?"

Laura gasped, making Henry blink
and look up at her. "Really?"

"Mm-hm. We could go to the
shelter over in Linmere. I know they
have lots of dogs looking for homes –
maybe not puppies as cute as Henry,
but I'm sure they're still gorgeous.
I could look after a dog while you're
at school. When I'm cleaning one of
the cottages, it could come and play in
the garden. I'm sure that would be all
right."

Laura nodded slowly. "I'd love to
have our own dog." She looked down at
Henry's silky head, flopped over her lap,
and let out a little sigh, although she did
her best to hide it from Mum.

She ought to be so happy and she was, she really was.

But it was so hard to think of loving another dog as much as she loved Henry.

Chapter Six

"I really love walking him," Laura
told Annie, as they wandered along
the beach together. Laura had popped
over to see if Henry wanted a walk,
and Annie had said she'd come, too.
"It's been so nice of you to let me," she
added.

Henry was darting over the damp
sand at the edge of the sea, making

squeaky yapping noises at the waves. "I took him down to the village with me yesterday, and everybody we met stopped and patted him. He had a fan club outside the sweet shop," Laura said, giggling as Henry glared fiercely at a pile of seaweed.

"I wish Molly and the others liked him as much you do," said Annie. "She still hasn't forgiven him for chewing up her bag." Then she sighed. "I'm not sure what's going to happen when I go off to uni, either. Mum and Dad said I could have a present for finishing my exams, and I'd wanted a puppy for so long… Mum said she'll look after him, but she isn't really a dog person. I hope he's going to be OK." She gave her shoulders a little shake and smiled at Laura. "I'm sure he will be, don't look so worried! Anyway, Laura, why don't you have a dog? You're brilliant with Henry! Is it that your mum's too busy?"

"Actually, she just said we could get a dog from the rescue centre! And it's all because of Henry. She said she could see how much I love him, and that maybe I should have a dog of my own." Laura didn't say that she and her mum thought they'd be better dog-owners than Annie, but she was sure it was true. How could Annie have asked for a puppy just a few months before she went away to university?

Annie nodded, looking thoughtful. "Your mum's right," she murmured. "Sorry, but we'd better head back now, Laura. I said I'd go to the shops for some crisps and things – we're having a party for Zara's birthday tonight."

Henry darted behind the sofa with his tail tucked between his legs. He wasn't sure what was going on. He'd been sleeping in his basket in the kitchen when Logan had tripped over it and nearly trodden on him. Logan had just groaned and laughed, and then

shoved the basket into the utility room.
Henry had decided to get out of the
way, but somehow the living room was
even busier than the kitchen. Everyone
seemed to be stomping around, and
the music was so loud it felt like the
house was shaking.

He peered round the arm of the
sofa and whined, looking for Annie.
He couldn't see her anywhere.
Uncertainly, he scurried along the
edge of the room, making for the
open door that led out to the garden.
He could smell the fresh air and the
sharp, salty tang of the sea. Perhaps
Annie was outside? Or maybe he'd
find Laura – he was sure her house was
somewhere nearby. He could curl up
and snuggle with her on her bed again.

That would be a much better place to sleep.

Henry nosed his way out into the dark garden…

"Laura? Are you awake, sweetheart?"

Laura sat up in bed. She was half awake. She'd been dreaming, and everything still felt strange and dreamlike now. The thudding sound of the music from her dream was still there. She shook her head, trying to shake it away, but it didn't help.

Laura blinked and rubbed her eyes, realizing at last that the music was real. And loud!

"What's going on?"

"The people from the farmhouse, again," Mum sighed. "I'm going to have to go and get them to turn the music off. It's one o'clock in the morning, for goodness' sake! I thought I'd better wake you up and tell you. I'll be back soon though, OK?"

Laura nodded and peered out of her window. The farmhouse was all lit up and she could see the shadows of people dancing against the curtains. The music was so loud her window seemed to be shaking.

"Henry!" Laura gasped, suddenly imagining the little dog shut in the house with all that noise. He must be terrified. She leaped out of bed, shoving her feet into her slippers and grabbing a hoody. Then she hurried down the stairs. Mum hadn't locked the front door, so Laura could just slip out behind her.

"What are you doing?" her mum asked, jumping as Laura touched her sleeve. "You gave me a fright, Laura. I didn't even hear you coming up behind me." She rolled her eyes. "I suppose that isn't a surprise, is it?"

"I just remembered about Henry," Laura explained. "I'm worried about him, Mum."

"Oh dear, I hadn't thought of that. Poor little dog!" Mum knocked on the door, and Laura stood next to her, huddled into her hoody. She hoped that Annie and her friends weren't going to be annoyed about being asked to turn off the music.

The yard looked so different in the dark, full of odd shadows and strange shapes. Laura caught her breath, her heart suddenly thumping as one of the shadows moved – and came slinking towards them. She grabbed her mum's arm with a squeak.

"What is it? Oh, honestly, are they never going to answer this door?"

"Mum, there's something…" The shadow settled into a little brown and white shape, padding across the yard. "Oh! Oh, Henry, it's you!" Laura gave a shaky laugh. For about half a second, she really had wondered if it was a ghost!

"Henry?" Mum turned round to look. "He's out here on his own?" Shaking her head crossly, she banged on the door again.

Laura scooped Henry up in her arms, hugging him tight. He licked her cheek and snuggled his head under her chin. "Did you slip out? Was it too noisy for you, too? Poor puppy! I wish I could just take you back to the cottage with me. I'd look after you."

She perched on the bench outside the farmhouse, loving the feel of the puppy in her arms, squirmy and soft. "I bet they haven't even noticed you've gone," she whispered in Henry's fluffy ear.

Then she sat up straighter, suddenly getting an idea. "Mum… Couldn't we just take Henry back home with us for the rest of the night? He's scared of the noise."

Mum shook her head sadly. "I wish we could, Laura. But don't worry, I'm going to make them turn the music down. Oh, at last!"

Someone had finally opened the door. One of the boys was standing there, peering out as though he was surprised to see Laura's mum. It was Logan, the one she'd seen taking Henry out that first day, Laura realized.

"Yes?" he said sullenly.

"Can you please turn that music off! Do you know what time it is?"

Laura's mum sounded really annoyed.

If it had been me, Laura thought,
*I would have done as I was told straight
away.* That was the kind of voice Mum
used when she was sending Laura to
her room. But Logan didn't seem to
care. He just kept saying that it wasn't
all that late. Laura could tell that her
mum was getting crosser by the second,
and she could feel Henry tensing up in
her arms.

"Come on," she muttered. "I'll have to take you back in a minute, but not till it's all sorted out. It isn't fair." She hurried round the corner of the farmhouse, where the angry voices weren't so clear, and stood there stroking Henry and murmuring to him.

"Oh!" The music went off, and the sudden silence was eerie. It sounded almost louder than the music had, and the night seemed darker all at once. Laura felt Henry wriggle in her arms. "I know, I suppose we ought to go back. I expect Mum's told them about you, too, by now." Reluctantly, Laura padded round the corner of the house.

"There you are!" Her mum sounded relieved.

"Sorry – Henry was scared." Laura came up to the door and looked at Logan. Several other people were behind him now, and Laura wished she'd stayed to support her mum. It must have been really hard having to tell them all what to do. None of them looked very happy.

Laura peered round Mum's shoulder. Annie didn't seem to be there, but she could see Annie's friend Molly.

Laura was just about to ask where Annie was, so she could give Henry back, when Molly stepped forward. "How did he get out here?" she asked. "I bet someone left that gate open again."

"We found him in the yard. He doesn't like loud noises and shouting…" Laura whispered, holding him out to Molly.

Molly
grabbed him,
but Henry
wriggled and
twisted, and
Molly squealed
and let go. He
landed heavily on
the floor with a yelp. Then he crept
back to Laura, whining and pressing
himself miserably against her legs.

Laura was gentle and friendly,
and her house was quiet. She played
with him, and took him for walks,
and didn't yank his lead to hurry him
up. Even when he was scared, like
tonight, Laura always protected him.
He slunk round behind Laura's fluffy
slippers and barked at the other girl.

He barked as loud as he could, but it came out as a shrill, frightened noise.

"Oh, stop it, you silly dog. Come here," Molly said, leaning down to grab him again.

Henry snapped his teeth at her crossly, just grazing the back of her hand. He didn't really mean to bite, but everything was just so scary.

"Hey!" Molly snatched her hand away with a gasp. "Ow! Bad dog!"

Henry heard Laura protest, but Molly picked him up again and marched into the house. Henry peered over her arm, scrabbling and whining and looking for Laura. He could still see her, leaning against her mum and crying. He clawed at the girl's sleeve, trying to wriggle free, but this time he couldn't get away.

"Naughty dog! No biting!" Molly
said, carrying him into the utility room
and dumping him down on the tiles.
"Just stay there!"

She slammed the door, and Henry
crouched in front of it, shaking
all over. He was all alone and so
frightened.

Whimpering, he turned round and
slunk across the floor to his basket. He
climbed in, pressing his head against
the soft side and burrowing half under
the crumpled blanket. He wanted to
hide himself away from everything.

Chapter Seven

"Are they really going to go home?
Even though they're supposed to stay
nearly another week?" Laura stared at
her mum. She felt like crying.

"They have to," Mum said with
a sigh. "I spoke to Jenny from the
letting agency this morning, after I'd
already had three different families
complaining to me about the noise.

She says she'll call them and explain that they've got to leave."

"Today?" Laura asked, her voice very small.

"I think so. Sorry, sweetheart." Mum hugged her. "But I expect Henry will be happy to go home. He hasn't liked being in a house full of people."

"We don't know what his home's like," Laura muttered into her mum's sleeve. "Maybe that's full of people, too. Annie might have loads of brothers and sisters." She couldn't help being down. She felt too miserable to look on the bright side. Her mum just hugged her tighter. She could tell how upset Laura was.

"Do you think I'll be able to say goodbye to him?" Laura said,

her voice still
muffled, so that
her mum had
to tilt her head
to listen.

"I hope so. I'll
have to go over to
pick up the keys and
make sure they've left the house nice
and tidy. You can come with me, if you
like. Although no one's going to be in
a very good mood," she warned.

Laura looked up and nodded,
biting her lip. She didn't really want
to listen to another argument like the
night before, but she couldn't miss the
chance to say goodbye.

"I'm glad you won't have to have
everybody complaining to you any

more," she said, resting her head against her mum's shoulder.

"Me, too. And, Laura, I really did mean it about us getting a dog. You've been so good at helping with Henry. Very responsible. Try and think of the positive things, OK?"

Laura nodded. She was trying. But all she could think of was Henry last night, whimpering as Molly carried him away.

Henry was sitting underneath the coffee table. He didn't really want to be there, but he didn't know where else to go. He'd been curled up on Annie's lap, enjoying being cuddled and fussed over, when the sharp sound of the doorbell had made him jump. And it had made everyone start shouting again. Annie had got up, leaving him on the sofa, but there was just too much noise to stay there. So he'd clambered down into the small, safe space under the table.

Perhaps he should go and sit in his basket? If he went to sleep for a while, maybe everything would quieten down again. Henry poked his nose out from under the table and then flinched back as a suitcase on wheels went rattling by. But then he shook himself briskly and went trotting out after the case. He wasn't going to sleep. He would go and find Laura, instead. They could go for a walk. Or even just snuggle up together, the way they had the other day.

Both of the times when he'd got out of the house before, he'd slipped out of the side gate in the garden, so he went that way again, keeping close to the walls and skittering past the piles of bags and beach stuff. Whenever he heard people come hurrying past, Henry froze. But no one seemed to notice him, anyway. The back door that led into the little garden was open, like it had been the night before, and Henry slipped out. His feathery tail started to wag delightedly to and fro. He would see Laura soon!

But the garden gate was closed. Henry sat in front of it, confused, his tail sweeping from side to side on the

dusty path. He had only ever seen it
open. This wasn't right. After a minute
or so, it was clear that the gate wasn't
going to move. He got up and sniffed
at it, and then stood up on his hind
paws and scrabbled away, but all it did
was creak a little and rattle. It stayed
very firmly shut.

Henry gave the gate one last hopeful look. Then he sniffed at the tall plants growing up beside the fence and peered between the slats. There was the path. That was the way Laura had always taken him. That path would take him back to her, he was sure.

Henry crept along the base of the fence, pushing his way through the thick stems and scratching half-heartedly at the wooden posts here and there. But the fence was solid, and the wooden slats were too close together even for a little dog to squeeze through. Henry slumped down under a clump of poppies, feeling helpless. His coat was tangled, and full of grass seeds and bits of twig. He was hot and cross – and he was still stuck. He sank his chin down on his paws and gazed miserably at the ground. Then his nose twitched thoughtfully.

Right in front of him, there was a small dip under the fence. It had started as nothing more than a puddle of rain dripping down from a bush, but the water had smoothed the earth away, and now there was a definite hollow. Almost big enough for a little dog to squirm through.

Henry sprang up with an excited whine, and began to scrape and scuff with his soft puppy claws at the dry earth. It only took a few minutes to widen the hole out and dig it a little deeper, and then deeper still... Until it was just big enough for him

to force his
head under.
He squeezed
and wriggled
and shoved until
he was outside on
the path.

Henry stared around triumphantly
and shook the dusty earth out of his
fur. Then he set off, his head held high,
to find Laura.

Laura stood next to her mum – as
close as she could. Laura wanted Mum
to know that she was right there beside
her. Logan was telling Mum that it
was completely unfair they were being

made to leave. Laura thought it wasn't fair that her mum just had to stand there and listen to people shouting at her again.

"Look, I can see that you're upset, but the best thing to do is to send an email to the letting agency," Mum said patiently.

Laura peered round Mum, trying to see into the other rooms. She wasn't sure where Henry was. She could see his basket in the utility room, but he wasn't in it. Maybe he was hiding somewhere, because of all the angry voices?

"I just need to check round the house to make sure that everything's tidy," Mum explained. "It looks like you're mostly packed up. Are you bringing the cars round to the front? You can put them in the yard for loading up, if you like."

Laura trailed after Mum round the upstairs rooms. The group were really going, any minute now. If she didn't find Henry soon, she wouldn't be able to say goodbye to him at all. Maybe Annie had taken him for a last walk, she thought sadly.

But then she saw Annie packing up stuff from one of the bathrooms. So that wasn't it. Wherever could he be? She longed to ask, but Annie looked unhappy about leaving, too, and Laura didn't want to make things any harder for Mum. She'd see Henry in a minute, as they were putting him in the car. Even if it was just for one last quick cuddle.

Chapter Eight

Henry peered round the corner of the farmhouse, eyeing the commotion going on in the yard. He wanted to see if he could find Laura, but a car had driven up, and then another one, both braking sharply and sending up a spray of gravel and dust.

A car door slammed and he flinched back. Maybe he wouldn't go this way.

Henry looked around nervously.
Perhaps Laura was at the beach? But
he wasn't sure he wanted to go further
down the clifftop path by himself.
Instead, he pattered a little way across
the gravel and crept in between two
large pots of flowers.

He'd sit here and watch
for Laura.
And then,
there she was!
Coming out of the
farmhouse – she had
been there all the time!
Henry yelped and
poked out his nose from
between the flowerpots. But then
a car door slammed again and there
were people everywhere, flinging bags

into the cars and shouting to each other. He didn't dare go past them. Henry wriggled back, deeper into the little damp space between the pots. The trailing leaves hid him and he felt quite safe, but he couldn't reach Laura...

Laura stood with her mum by the front door of the farmhouse, looking at the two cars. Neither of them had space for a proper travel crate for a dog, she noticed. She couldn't even see any room for Henry to sit. If they put him in the boot with all those bags, one of them could easily topple over and squash him.

"Mum," she said, tugging at her mum's sleeve. "I still haven't seen Henry. He wasn't in the house."

Her mum glanced down at her. "Wasn't he? I suppose I didn't see him, either…"

Just then, Annie came hurrying out of the front door, her face pale under her tan. "Has anyone seen Henry?" she asked. "I still can't find him and I've been looking for ages!"

"I thought he was shut in the utility room," Logan called back. "You said you wanted to keep him out of the way while we were packing."

"Yes, I know. But he isn't there now," Annie said. "The front door's wide open. And so's the back one."

Laura glanced worriedly at her

mum. Maybe Henry had gone down to the beach on his own. He could be *anywhere*.

"Yeah, but the garden gate's shut, isn't it?" Molly straightened up, frowning. She'd been shoving bags into one of the cars and now she pushed her hair out of her eyes, looking grumpy and hot. "He escaped that way the other times, so we've all been really careful about keeping it closed today."

"Then where is he?" Annie wailed. "He's not in the house. I've checked everywhere, under all the beds. I even went through all the cupboards. He must have got out."

Logan closed the boot of the car with a thump – it only just shut, the car was so packed.

"Not even sure we can fit him in the car," he called to Annie. "Maybe you should just leave him behind."

Laura stared at him in horror. She thought he must be joking – surely he had to be? But he wasn't smiling.

She clenched her fists, suddenly furious. How dare he?

"You can't just leave Henry behind. It's because of people like you that there are shelters full of abandoned dogs!" Laura yelled at him. "How can you say that? You don't even know where he is! He could be lost on the cliff, or down on the beach." Then she drew back against her mum, feeling her cheeks redden.

Logan shrugged, but he looked embarrassed, too. "I didn't actually mean we'd leave him…" he muttered.

"Of course I'm not leaving him!" Annie gulped. It seemed as though she was about to cry. "Laura, do you really think he could have gone all the way down to the beach?"

Laura nodded. "He loves it there."

"Well, don't be too long." Logan folded his arms, leaning against the car.

"I'll come and help look." Laura started to follow Annie, then glanced back at her mum to check it was OK.

"Yes, you'd better," her mum said. "I'll come, too, once I've got the keys."

Laura followed Annie along the front of the house, to the corner where the path started. She was trying to think of

118

all the places Henry might be. Where had he specially liked when they'd been out on walks? Maybe he was digging around in one of those piles of smelly seaweed on the beach again.

Then something made her glance sideways, down at the flowerpots. Perhaps it was a tiny whimper, or perhaps a scuffling of puppy claws.

He was there – gazing out at her. Laura could see his tail, wagging just a little, as though he wasn't quite sure whether to be happy. He didn't want to come out, she guessed. Too much shouting and banging and general horribleness.

Laura stopped. She'd have to tell Annie, of course. Only … if she didn't, maybe they would go without him, like Logan had said. Maybe they'd leave Henry, and she could keep him… Laura dug her fingernails into her palms, hesitating.

But she couldn't say nothing, even though she wanted to, so much.

Laura took a deep breath and called after Annie, who was just disappearing round the corner of the house. "He's here!"

"Henry!" Annie came dashing over, her footsteps crunching on the gravel. But the puppy edged backwards, further into the space between the pots.

"I think he's scared," Laura said sadly. She glanced round and saw that Mum had hurried up beside her. She looked sad, too.

"Come on, Henry," Annie called.

"Can't you just grab him?" Logan yelled.

Annie turned round to glare at him. "Shut up, Logan! He doesn't like people shouting – you're making it worse. Come on, Henry…"

Laura kneeled down in front of the pots and looked in at the puppy. "Henry," she whisper-called. "It's OK. Come on out."

Henry eyed her and then glanced at Annie. Very slowly, he started to creep towards them, paw by paw, as though he wasn't sure if he was doing the right thing. He then made a sudden little rush and jumped at Laura, scrambling on to her lap. He was shivering and Laura wrapped her arms around him.

She stood up slowly and rubbed her cheek against his soft fur one last time. Then, reluctantly, she held him out to Annie.

Annie looked at her for a moment. At last she shook her head. "No…" she said quietly. "No. I think you'd better keep him. You'll look after him a lot better than I have."

"W-what?" Laura stammered. She'd

wished and wished for Annie to say just that. Now she thought she might have imagined it.

"Keep him. He can be yours, if you like."

"Hang on…" Laura's mum shook her head. "That's really nice of you, but he must have been an expensive puppy. I don't think we can take him."

"Oh, Mum!" Laura gasped, her eyes filling with tears. "Please…" She'd been so happy, just for a second.

But Annie smiled – a stiff, unhappy sort of smile. "I shouldn't ever have asked for him, it was really selfish. He'll be much happier with you." She sighed and put out her hand to stroke Henry's soft ears. "I'll miss you," she murmured.

"Well…" Laura's mum frowned. "I suppose, if you're sure."

"So, I can keep him?" Laura asked, in a whisper.

Mum nodded. "Yes!"

Annie turned away sharply, and grabbed Henry's basket and bowls and food out of the car. She pushed them into Mum's arms and then dived into the front seat as though she wanted to get away as quickly as possible.

Laura stood watching as the cars backed slowly out of the yard. Henry was still in her arms – they were going, really going, and leaving Henry behind with her. She stared down at him anxiously. Would he be upset, seeing Annie leave? But he looked quite happy snuggled up against her T-shirt.

"I've got a dog!" she said to Mum, only half believing it. Was this all just some kind of dream?

"You have!" Mum agreed, her eyes wide. "Oh my goodness! We've got a dog…" She glanced at the basket and bowls and bag of food she was holding, and shook her head slightly. "I suppose we'd better go and put these inside."

As Laura followed her mum back into the house, Henry licked her ear, making her giggle. She couldn't be dreaming, if her ear was all wet… She stood in the hall with Henry, kicking off her flip-flops, and watched Mum hang the puppy's red lead on one of the coat hooks.

"It looks perfect," Laura whispered in Henry's ear. "It looks just like you belong!"

HOLLY WEBB

Holly Webb started out as a children's book editor and wrote her first series for the publisher she worked for. She has been writing ever since, with over one hundred books to her name. Holly lives in Berkshire, with her husband and three children. Holly's pet cats are always nosying around when she is trying to type on her laptop.

For more information
about Holly Webb visit:

www.holly-webb.com